WALT

Walt

IAN STOBA

Auslander & Fox
Los Angeles, CA

Published in 2012 by Auslander & Fox.

Auslander & Fox
P.O. Box 25322
Los Angeles, CA 90025
www.auslanderandfox.com

This book is printed on acid free, sustainably-sourced paper.

The layout is by Martin Wallace, and the cover is by Jana Vukovic.

ISBN 978-1-936117-82-6

No lobsters were harmed in the manufacture of this book.

DEDICATION

This book is for the cast and crew of the 37 Corbett, San Francisco Municipal Railway, and also for MMS (of course).

I

WALT LEANED OUT OVER the gunnel of his boat and reached into the water. His hand wrapped around the wet hemp line and began to pull.

Fishing for lobsters, called crawfish by the locals, has been a way of life on Tristan de Cunha for hundreds of years. Walt's family had been fishing these selfsame waters for seven generations.

Pulling up a lobster trap was not a new thing for Walt.

After loading his day's catch onto his narrow wooden boat, Walt rowed to the dock of the Processing Plant. The Plant was the center of industry on the tiny island, the place to which all crawfish were brought. There they were scientifically killed and their tails were removed and preserved by means of deep freezing for their long journeys to the restaurants and dining tables of the world.

Walt himself had never tasted lobster. As far as he knew, not one individual in the seven generations of Tristanian lobster fishermen in Walt's family had ever tasted a lobster. Curiously, he had never even wondered what a crawfish tail might taste like. This was just as well for him as no one on the island, not even the foreman of the Plant, who had been brought from England, could afford to buy a lobster.

Just as curiously, I myself had never tasted lobster at that point, and in fact still never have. Although, as may be seen by and by, my reasons were, and are, altogether different from Walt's.

Only one small item interrupted Walt's afternoon, one point of malaise intruded into his brain: for the third straight day now Walt had been hearing music in his head. The same song had been playing nonstop inside his skull, closer in than his ears somehow, as if he was not really hearing it but somehow feeling it vibrate in his jaws and cheekbones.

Walt was becoming just the slightest bit concerned. He had had difficulty sleeping last night because of this strange music, so unlike anything played on Tristan, that played nonstop inside his head. The sound was metallic and thin. He was aware of a voice but could not hear the words. What he perceived most clearly was the sound of an electric guitar, one played in a manner he had never heard before. The sound was odd, drifting into atonality in bits and often seeming a little off, yet still fitting somehow.

Walt had never been particularly curious or imaginative. Perhaps if he had, he would have paid more attention to this strange music, and he might even have wondered what was causing it. As it was, his fisherman's interest was only in finding out what piece of music it was, since he was certain that he could not have made it up. Walt was not a composer, he was a fisherman.

Having rid himself of the day's catch at the Plant, Walt resolved to go see Mrs. Wilkins, the island's only piano teacher. Walt of course had never studied music; his family considered him far too simple-minded for such things. Walt's only real tie to Mrs. Wilkins was that he had once courted her daughter Leonore. Leonore worked in Tristan's other great industry: postage stamps. Tristanian stamps are valued by collectors all over the world for their beauty and rarity.

As with most means of employment, the reality of the Tristanian Postal Service, Philatelic Bureau, was not nearly as glamorous as it sounds. Leonore was one of four women who licked each beautiful stamp, stuck it to a first day card, canceled the stamp by hand with an ancient postal implement, and finally sent it on its way over the ocean to a stranger eager for the rare and beautiful stamp.

In retrospect, Walt's courtship now seemed to him doomed from the beginning. He and Leonore had little in common but hormones, and did not even really enjoy each other's company very much. It was an extremely rare burst of imagination on Walt's part which brought them together at all. Entirely out of character, and all by himself, he had imagined that women who licked things for a living might have mysterious erotic powers. The idea took hold of him until he could scarcely think of anything else during the long hours he spent one each day in his little boat.

As the other three stamp-lickers were already married, he had no alternative but to pursue Leonore or perhaps die wondering about her tongue. She herself did not seem overly enthusiastic about Walt. It took him some time to convince her that he was indeed serious about marrying her. It took some time after their initial encounter for her to do anything but run to her house and hide at the slightest hint of Walt's proximity.

His curiosity remained strong, though, and ultimately overcame her repugnance. She never actually agreed to marry Walt, but she did after some time become civil, and finally affectionate. This was the undoing of their romance; finally, after months of wondering, pursuing and fantasizing, Walt actually kissed Leonore. Her mouth tasted like paste. Her tongue was swollen and covered in cuts from the serrated edges of the stamps.

After their first, and only, kiss, Walt told Leonore that he was breaking off the engagement and wanted nothing more to do with her. Walt then walked down to the beach where his boat was kept, threw himself into it bodily and sobbed. If he had looked back towards Leonore's house, which he didn't, he would have seen her stand there for a long moment before walking away, confused.

Walt remembered all these things as he walked up the familiar path to the house that Leonore shared with her mother, Mrs. Wilkins. He remembered, too, the times that he had run to the house breathlessly behind Leonore, only to see her flee inside the door, slam it, then run to the windows and slam shut the shutters.

As much as he wanted to speak to Mrs. Wilkins, he felt the he was not ready just yet to face Leonore again.

So, with no better idea coming to him at the moment, he decided to walk home.

Walt lived in a shack. The walls had been built from

the planks of a sailing ship that had run aground off Tristan sometime in the mid-eighteenth century. Time since then had allowed gaps to open between the planks so that Walt, if he were so inclined, could peek out unobserved from any of at least a dozen spots in his little home.

His housetop was a comical imitation of a roof. Sometimes he felt that it let in more rain than it kept out. Most of Walt's pots and all three of his pans, as well as all but one of his cups, were spread on the floor in an unsuccessful battle against the besieging rain. Next to Walt's canvas cot was stacked a rather large and messy pile of sweaters. The climate of Tristan leaned heavily in the direction of cold and wet, so that Walt, with his creaking and leaking little shack, found that he always had to wear at least two sweaters to bed. Now that he was home and feeling the chill of the wind more than when he had been out, he pulled a grey wool sweater over the two similar ones he was already wearing. The continual dampness combined with Walt's penchant for decaying wool sweaters gave the shack a smell very much like that of a wet sheepdog.

Walt built a fire in his wood-burning stove that provided heat as well as a cooking surface for the shack. With the music in his head still playing nonstop, he prepared a meager supper.

Composing himself, he carried a steaming plate of less savory parts of fish to his simple table. The music was really beginning to get to him now. He remembered his sleeplessness the previous night and wondered what would happen when he tried to lie down on his cot tonight. He took a bite of his food. He had a thought that would no doubt have occurred to most people sooner: he wondered if he could be losing his mind. The enormity of this thought took Walt so much by surprise that he dropped his fork. Fortunately for Walt he did not know that one of the earliest and most accurate signs of impending madness is that one may feel that he is losing his mind.

He picked up his fork. He carefully drew and released three deep breaths. He then took another bite of his supper. The music continued to play in his head. Calmly, more calmly than he could ever have imagined himself doing so, he picked up his plate and threw it across the room. The plate hit the wall with a satisfying thwack and a clang. The plate, being metal, was not damaged beyond a few minor dents, but the assorted parts of fish made an impressive display on the wall.

Walt strode the four strides it took him to cross the room and stood facing his steamer trunk. The trunk, salvaged from another shipwreck, this one around 1880, provided storage for Walt's few possessions. He opened the hasp and lifted the lid. He brought out two bottles from inside the trunk, one of port and the other of rum.

Walt was not one to drink. In fact, he could not remember the last time he had had anything to drink besides water and the strong tea that he brewed on winter mornings. He remembered that the port had been a gift. He had once accidentally saved a man from drowning. The man had fallen off another boat and had gotten his leg fouled in one of the lines leading to Walt's lobster traps. Looking to see what he had caught that day, he was very surprised to find a saturated Tristanian fisherman and no lobsters. To the end of his days on Earth, Walt maintained that the flailing of the overboard fisherman had scared away all the lobsters that day.

The man was, of course, grateful to be saved. It is a tradition on Tristan, as in most places, to be grateful to a person who saves one's life, and to show that appreciation in the form of gifts. The problem was, no one was quite sure what Walt liked or what it was that he might want. So, by default, the man with a continued opportunity to be alive gave Walt a blue wool sweater, which was enjoyed immensely; a black wool cap, which went overboard the very first time Walt tried to wear it fishing; and this bottle of port which had lain unopened in Walt's steamer trunk for some years now.

He also recalled the genesis of his bottle of rum. He had actually bought it for himself the day he got his own boat. This was also the day his father, to whom the boat had previously belonged, had died. One of the few things that Walt could bring to mind about his father was a saying of his to the effect that anyone old enough to have his own fishing boat was old enough to drink rum. This saying was repeated to Walt's mother on an almost nightly basis whenever she complained about the old fisherman's drinking. It was so ingrained into Walt's impressionable thought process that it was the most natural thing in the world for him to buy a bottle of rum with the money from the first catch he delivered all by himself to the Plant. And with just as little thought, he had delivered that bottle to his steamer trunk where it had remained up until this very moment.

Only with extreme difficulty was Walt able to uncork the bottles. Of course he had no bottle opener. He was forced to make creative use of a thin knife usually reserved for cleaning fish. He made a mess of it, shredding the corks into so many pieces that they could never hope to reseal the bottles, and dropping showers of cork fragments onto the floor and into each of the liquors.

So, trying to put out the music in his head, Walt, for the very first time in his life, got drunk.

The quantity Walt drank that night would be enough to level the most experienced drunk. A whole bottle of rum and another of port were consumed within the space of an hour and a half. Although he had no idea at the time, that amount of alcohol could easily have killed Walt or caused irreparable brain damage. As it was, he lapsed into a coma that was only temporary.

Walt awoke in a most peculiar position. He was lying down on his stomach on his cot with his head hanging over the edge. He had no memory of putting himself in that position. He was fortunate that he had, though, as almost any other contortion of his body would have resulted in him choking on his vomit, which now covered nearly the entire floor of the shack.

Walt's vocabulary contained no words for how he felt. No hyperbolic extension of "hangover" could come close to the feeling of desolation in his body. If had cared to, he might have compared his body to a city that has been ransacked and looted in time of war, abandoned by the invading troops after everything of any possible interest had been consumed or broken or violated.

It was doubtful that Walt possessed such imagery even at the best of times. Now, even the thought of speech was far beyond his capabilities. The only thing that he knew for certain was that he needed water desperately.

Painfully he stood up. He fell immediately, face first into a pool of vomit which oozed through all three of his sweaters and made his skin tingle. Unable to stand, he crawled through the muck to the basin where he kept water.

He dipped ladle into basin and sipped the cool clear water. He felt his strength returning with each sip. Impulsively he took a deep drink, and immediately started vomiting again. If anything, he now felt worse than before, and worse still when he remembered the sensation of being drunk. He was indifferent to the drunkenness itself, it was the music that scared him. Instead of numbing the effects of the endlessly repeating music as he had hoped, the drink amplified the sound until it echoed back on itself in his head. With each passing moment, as the sound grew worse and worse, he could think of no other remedy but to drink more.

His vision failed him long before he passed into unconsciousness, but in those moments before exhaustion and alcohol poisoning carried him into a parody of restful sleep, in a sense beyond, or below, vision, he became aware of a spiral and felt its emptiness in the darkness.

When he was finally able to walk, he struck out for Mrs. Wilkins' house. As soon as he came with sight of the house he heard a shriek from inside, soon followed by the familiar sound of the slamming of the shutters.

He forced himself up the two steps to the porch and to the front door. Even in his current state he knew that knocking would be useless. He called out to the house as loud as he was able, which was not very loud at all, that it was Mrs. Wilkins that he was here to see, that he was not interested in marrying Leonore anymore and, for that matter was not interested in Mrs. Wilkins as a spouse either. Only when he said that he had a problem to do with music did he hear any response inside the house. Cautious footsteps now edged down the hall and toward the door. Finally the door opened a crack.

Mrs. Wilkins' face peered out at him with an odd mixture of revulsion and pity. She asked him what could possibly have worked him up to such a state. He was unable to answer. Finally, hesitantly, she invited him inside.

Walt had never been good with words, and now he faced attempting something that was for him nearly impossible: explaining to a woman he felt his superior by so much that she must be scarcely able to understand his speech that music was driving him crazy. He managed to get across to her that he was now in the fourth day of a continual and involuntary listening session. He said that he had gotten drunk, or that the music had gotten him drunk, and that the worst part of the whole thing, the only reason he had come to her rather than diving off his boat with a bucket of rocks tied around his neck, was that he did not even know what the music was. The only thing that he was sure of was that, even though he was not familiar with the music before it started playing in his head, it was not if his invention. He was convinced that it was, as he said, real music; that is, actually played by someone.

Before we come around to Mrs. Wilkins' response to this foul-smelling wretch who had appeared at her door, it is important that we share some basic background information about her. A brief biography is very much in order.

She was born on Tristan, February 13, 1948. She endured a relatively uneventful childhood, unusual only in the interest she had in music. From the time she was in the third grade, she would wake up early and get to school an hour before classes started so that she could play what was then the only piano on the island.

During the 1960's many Tristanian parents felt that their children should have opportunities beyond fishing, working in the Plant, or licking stamps. For the first time in generations, young people were given the chance to leave the island to study. Nearly all of the students went to England since, due to some obscure diplomatic resolution, all Tristanians are able to travel on British passports.

Mrs. Wilkins, then simply known as Miss Wilkins, won a scholarship to Cambridge to study music. Once there, she rapidly became involved in the growing counterculture movement. She became fascinated, even obsessed, with the various forms of popular music then fashionable. The psychedelic music coming out of San Francisco at that point particularly grabbed her. Her favorite band was Strawberry Alarm Clock. Hoping to emulate their style, she formed a group of her own called Breakfast All Over.

Breakfast All Over's best-known song "Eat it For Breakfast" rose as high as number seventeen on some British singles charts. Success was short lived: the band broke up soon after "Eat it" peaked on the charts, apparently because of an inability to decide which guru to follow.

After the breakup of the band, things only got worse for Miss Wilkins. Her thesis "Structural and Motivic Analysis of the Music of Strawberry Alarm Clock" was unanimously rejected by her department at Cambridge. She was forced to leave the University.

She decided to return to Tristan, hoping to be able to somehow make a living teaching music. Remembering her own difficulties in finding a piano to practice on, she spent most of the money that she had made with Breakfast All Over on a Steinway, which she had shipped to Tristan. The rest of the money she spent on a huge stereo system and an enormous collection of recordings, including at least five copies of everything Strawberry Alarm Clock had ever played. It was perhaps the largest private collection of psychedelic music ever assembled. This, too, was shipped back to Tristan.

Finally, she had herself shipped back to Tristan.

By the way, it was sometime during her stay in England that Leonore was born. Only Mrs. Wilkins knew for sure who the father was, but all she would say was that he was someone famous.

For years one of the most popular pastimes for Tristanians on rainy days was to speculate about who Leonore's father could be. Many thought it was the Prince of Wales, whom she slightly resembled. Others, who had some awareness of music from Mrs. Wilkins' record collection, thought it might be Jimi Hendrix, whom Leonore also resembled slightly. It was Tristan's favorite mystery and it seemed that the answer would never be known for sure.

By the way, when she returned to the island with her piano and her thousands of records and reels of tape and her daughter, she announced to everyone that from now on she would be called Mrs. Wilkins and that she would now be their music teacher. Tristanians are overwhelmingly agreeable people and they willingly enough complied with her wishes.

All these things flashed through Walt's mind in the long moment during which she stared at him in fixed concentration, then audibly drew her breath in through her teeth. She stood up hesitantly, telling him to wait in the parlor, she would be back.

II

WHILE MRS. WILKINS is out of the room, it might be an opportune time to remind the reader that this story is not about Walt alone. I am as much a part of it as is Walt, or Mrs. Wilkins, or even Jose, King of the Parking Lot, whom you have not yet met.

At about the time that our Mrs. Wilkins was searching through her three rooms of scratched and outdated recordings, I was descending from the roof of the apartment building in which I live. The building is at the corner of Ninth and Folsom streets in San Francisco. San Francisco is over seven thousand miles from the beaches and lobster pots of Tristan de Cunha.

What was I doing on the roof? I was checking the automatic transmitter, which I had built. I found it to be in perfect working order.

I walked casually down the steps. The first flight was bare wood, and so echoed under my feet. The other flights were carpeted and much less noisy. On the second floor, I stopped off at my apartment to check the antenna.

Building the actual transmitter had not really been a problem. Scavenging the parts was less difficult than I had expected. My only difficulty had been finding a suitable antenna. I needed a large and well-formed piece of high quality metal that would transmit my signal through the universe.

My solution had been staring me in the face. Like some kind of Zen paradox, I had missed the answer because it was right in front of me.

The frame of my Bosendorfer Imperial grand piano, which took up, and still takes up, about 90% of the floor space of my apartment, is about the best broadcast antenna imaginable. And it was already here. All I had to do was drop a signal wire from the transmitter down the side of the building, through my window, and attach it to one of the bolts on the capo bar.

I found the antenna, too, to be in perfect working order.

I decided that I should check the piano in its function as a piano, as well as being an antenna. I found it to work marvelously.

I do not really play the piano in any conventional sense of the word. I remember when I was in second grade, every Friday was talent day. The classes would get together and sit on the floor while the kids who at that young age thought themselves to be talented did their respective things.

There was one boy whose name I do not remember. Every single Friday he would sit at the decrepit upright piano and play "The Entertainer". If there are nine months in a school year, that means that he played that same piece thirty-six times, every Friday without fail. For no reason was he ever sick or out on a religious holiday on a Friday.

At first I sort of envied him. I could play nothing on the piano or anything else, and he could at least play one thing. After a while I began to experience a subtle shift of feeling, perhaps the first time in my young life that I had sustained an emotional evolution. I grew to despise that kid, to dread school on Fridays, to malign the pompousness that would allow a seven year old to have so limited a repertoire, and be so blasted proud of it. I decided at some point that I would learn to play something on the piano, and it would be something better than his "Entertainer".

And I did.

Today I can play Hindemith's Second Piano Sonata. I can play at by memory. I can play it by touch in the dark, which I often do. I play it at all hours of the day and night.

It is the only thing I can play.

Undoubtedly, that boy who so aggravated me by playing the same piece over and over every Friday is no longer seven. He has gone off into the world somewhere. It is very likely that he no longer remembers his Friday glories of his youth. Or, perhaps, on drunken Thanksgivings, coaxed by family members; then, perhaps coaxed is not the right word: they ask him to play knowing that he will play whether they like it or not, this being a ritual of Thanksgiving, and they, being family, will do the right, nice, and honorable thing in asking him to play his fumbling version of that Joplin rag, if only to make him feel better, to make him feel that they like it, even; and if they are truly a religious family, they might say a collective prayer under their collective breath that, thank God, Thanksgiving only comes once a year, and this is the only time on the current journey around the sun that they have to appease this tipsy mediocrity.

Satisfied that all was well in my apartment, I went down the steps and on about my business.

I went out through the heavy glass front door of the building, pausing to check my mail. I was somewhat annoyed that the first day card I had ordered from Tristan de Cunha had not arrived yet. I turned left on Ninth Street and walked up to Market Street. Here I turned left and walked until I found the familiar steps down into the earth which announced a Station of the San Francisco Municipal Railway. For eighty-five cents I could ride the N Judah train back and forth as long as I wanted. I spent many afternoons shuttling endlessly between the Ferry Building at one extreme, and the Pacific Ocean at the other. Thinking, always thinking. There existed no less expensive, or more expansive, form of solitude in all the City.

There, you are all reminded. Now, please do not let me stray too far from your mind in all this about Walt and Tristan. I shall fade back into the wings of this story now, for I don't want to keep poor Mrs. Wilkins waiting.

Oh, before I go, I should note that Tristan de Cunha is the most remote spot on this planet that we call home. It is more than two thousand miles from any other bit of land big enough to stand on and habitable by human beings. Some writers who have never visited the island imagine it to be the loneliest place on Earth.

III

W HEN SHE RETURNED it was with an enormous arm-
load of records. She had determined that the music
playing in Walt's head was within her particular field of
specialization. She felt that, on the basis of what Walt had
said, she could safely narrow the choices down to about
two hundred possibilities, all but two of which were in her
collection. The thirty or so records under her arm com-
prised what she felt to be the most likely candidates.

For the next three hours Mrs. Wilkins was like the
wind. She threw records on the turntable, playing a few
seconds of each at maximum volume until Walt shook
his head no, signaling her to tear it off the still-turning
platform, more often than not scratching the record in the
process.

They covered a huge range of music. Walt had been
fairly sure that the words were in English, so she had
concentrated primarily on British and American groups.
Others gradually made their way into the mix though;
Canadian bands, South African bands, groups from all
over the Caribbean, the Philippines, Asian Bands, South-,
East-, and Central-European bands. Even one power trio

from Uruguay that did a few numbers in English did not escape.

As the hours wore on, Walt found himself feeling worse and worse. He experienced in the extreme the displacement any listener feels on hearing two dissimilar pieces of music played at once. The ever-changing audio barrage thrown at him by Mrs. Wilkins frightened him. In contrast, the music in his head seemed serenely safe and familiar. Of course he did not know what it was, that was what he was here to find out, but it was beginning to feel almost a part of him.

He was also beginning to feel faint. It took some time until he realized that this was from hunger. Judging from the looks of his shack, he had last night vomited up everything he had eaten for the last several weeks, as well as several vital internal organs. He knew he was already strained far beyond the few social skills he had mastered. He knew of no way to ask Mrs. Wilkins for food and, unless he went out on his boat today, which he knew he was totally incapable of doing, he would have no fish to eat or any money to buy other food.

The aural vertigo conspired with the cacophony in his body. He felt himself swaying involuntarily from side to side. His shoulders slipped forward. His vision became grey, then black around the edges. He knew that he was about to lose consciousness again.

As he pitched forward from his chair down to the floor he heard a sound. If he had had the musical vocabulary he would have known that it was a very familiar electric guitar repeatedly sounding the interval of a major third. As it was, all he knew was that it was the beginning of the cycle of the endlessly repeating music in his head. He wondered if it could just be an echo in his mind of the music that tormented him. As he lay face down on the floor, his weight on his right shoulder with his still-vomit-saturated sweaters making squishy noises on the planking, he realized that the same music was coming from the speakers as from inside his head. For the first time he was hearing this music with his ears.

He managed a wordless scream to Mrs. Wilkins over the music. Somehow he was suddenly on his feet, arms out at angles he did not understand, dancing stiff-legged around the room.

He crashed around the room, breaking several small items swept from tables and countertops. He crashed into walls, leaving putrid stains. He shouted that this was the right music, that he knew he had been right all along: he could not have made up this music, it belonged to someone else.

Then he did faint.

IV

WALT WOKE UP AFTER an indefinite amount of time. He was lying in a feather bed, with real blankets, and with an actual pillow under his head. In his own shack he used only tattered tarpaulins and fishing nets for bedding and a bundle of sweaters that refused to adhere to his body any longer on which to rest his head.

Mrs. Wilkins was gently dabbing his forehead with a moist facecloth. As his eyes began to focus, he saw that he was in a place which he had before seen only through the window: Leonore's bedroom. Leonore herself was nowhere to be seen.

Walt felt weaker then at any previous moment in his life. Mrs. Wilkins explained to him that he had been unconscious for three days. He opened his mouth and tried to speak, but found his tongue welded to his palate with dried mucous. As he had expected, the music continued to play in his head.

Mrs. Wilkins dipped the cloth into a basin of water and squeezed a few drops onto Walt's tongue. The relief was immense. When he was able to speak he told her that he was very thirsty, and hungry too. She left him to rest and went out to the kitchen.

She returned a few minutes later with weak tea, toast, and a soft boiled egg. She actually fed him part of the egg with a spoon and held the teacup for him until he was strong enough to sit up.

When Walt was able to pull himself up to a sitting position, he took over feeding himself. With every bite he felt his strength, and his hunger, increasing. By the time he had eaten all the toast he was ravenous. He asked Mrs. Wilkins to please bring him more food. He licked the plate the toast had been on. Mrs. Wilkins hurried out of the bedroom.

She was gone longer this time. Walt's stomach was roaring. He chewed his knuckles, his bedsheet, he would have chewed the sole of his rubber boots if he had been able to locate them.

Finally, after an impossible length of time, Mrs. Wilkins returned, heavily laden with food. She had a large bowl of oatmeal, four pancakes, thick slices of homemade bread, a whole pot of stronger tea, a jar of berry jam that she had made herself the previous spring, and three eggs, scrambled.

Walt spread the plates far and wide over the bed. He sampled each one in turn. He played games, eating two bites from each plate moving in a clockwise direction, then four bites from each in a counter-clockwise direction. Soon enough the food was gone. Walt was anything but full. Mrs. Wilkins now looked truly terrified. She ran out of the room, then out of the house. Walt heard the front door bang behind her.

He stayed in bed, not knowing what else to do. He lay on the edge of sleep when Mrs. Wilkins returned with three neighbor women. All of them carried large trays of food. Walt lost track of the things he was eating. He stopped noticing tastes and textures. His hands were a blur of motion, spooning brown liquids, stabbing green things with a fork, picking up everything with his hand and forcing it into his mouth. He ate the way he had once seen a group of sharks eat a pair of seals into a bloody nothingness.

When he stopped to breathe and look up, he saw that the women were covered in spray. As he raised his eyes to meet theirs, the neighbor ladies turned as one and ran screaming out of the house. Only Mrs. Wilkins remained by his side, and she was looking awfully perplexed and more than a little worried. She asked him if he had had enough to eat and he replied that he was in fact feeling quite full now.

Full yes, but not satisfied. Mrs. Wilkins still had not told him what the music was. He asked her. She seemed perplexed, her wandering mind showed through her eyes.

After a pause of several seconds that a better educated Walt would have recognized as a symptom of shock, her head snapped on her neck: she had realized what he was talking about.

She told him that he had responded to a recording by the Easybeats. Even with her vast knowledge of the music of that era of human history, she was unaware of any other recordings of this group. It was as if they had banded together for the exclusive purpose of one song, then disappeared off the face of the earth. However, she added that their one song, "Friday on my Mind", was a masterpiece, perhaps among the five best works to come out of the entire movement.

From Mrs. Wilkins this was extraordinarily high praise. Not only was she the world's foremost authority on the music of the 1960's, her personal tastes would have led her to attribute to Strawberry Alarm Clock at least four of the top five spots. In any case, she liked the Easybeats.

Walt felt relief in finally having a name for the sounds in his head. It was odd somehow; knowing what the music was did not change its being in his head, but somehow made it much easier to bear. The worry was greatly lessened. For example, he now had absolutely no desire to get drunk. He knew that the music would not keep him awake torturously as it had before. In giving it a name, he felt that he could perhaps live with it.

He finally asked a question which would have no doubt have occurred to most people much sooner: where was Leonore? She had been conspicuously absent during the almost four days that Walt had been in the Wilkins home.

By the way, "conspicuously" is my word and not Walt's. It is very doubtful that he could have pronounced a word with that many twisty vowels and syllables. Forgive me, I intrude again. I realize that I need not remind the reader so often of my existence, yet the urge is overpowering.

Mrs. Wilkins said that Leonore had been nervous seeing Walt approach the house again after such a long period of absence. She had initially retreated to the room that they were now in. That would, of course, account for the familiar clang of the slammed shutters that Walt had heard as he approached the house. She added that Leonore had stayed many hours at Walt's side during his period of catatonic sleep and had been called away shortly before he woke to the home of an elderly maiden aunt for whom she frequently did mending. Mrs. Wilkins attributed Leonore's initial fear of Walt's return to her girlish immaturity and skittishness, qualities which she was no longer young enough to properly claim.

Of course, this account was only partially true. She could not be expected to tell Walt the entire story of what had happened while he was dead to the world, but even Walt might find fault with the credibility of a story as thin as this one.

One perceptive, if intrusive, question he could have asked was this: just what sort of emergency seamstressing task could have taken as long as Leonore had been gone, especially when the owner of the wardrobe involved was a seventy year old Tristanian virgin of, at best, moderate means?

But Walt did not ask this, or any, question. Instead, he said that he felt that he was well enough to go home now. He thanked Mrs. Wilkins as best he could, pushed back the blankets and stood up to discover, and display, that his pants were missing.

Mortified, Walt dove head-first back into the bed, beneath the covers. He curled himself into a fetal position, feeling the intensity of the blush on his face and hearing the blood pound in his ears.

Walt felt a shame more profound than any feeling he

had ever imagined to be within the realm of human emotion. He wished that he did not have to endure the minutes that he felt must follow. He rocked gently back and forth, wishing destruction upon the world, hoping that he would never have to see Mrs. Wilkins again.

Mrs. Wilkins observed this scene with a look a knowing amusement. For the first time during the course of this narrative, she smiled. She turned lightly on her heel and left the room feeling years younger than she had just days before.

V

WALT REMAINED UNDER the bed for the rest of the day. Periodically, whenever his boredom made him think that the sun had set already, he very gently and quietly stuck one toe out from under the blankets. He felt that if his toes sensed cool, it would be night and he could escape from the house without having to see, or be seen by, Mrs. Wilkins.

At last his toe gave him the impression that the earth had turned. He lifted a corner of the blanket and risked a peak. It was indeed dark, he did not know how late. His eyes were well adjusted from the hours spent in hiding, and the fresh air was a tremendous relief. He breathed deeply, but quietly. He located his pants and pulled them on as quietly as possible.

Has it yet been noted that Walt did not so much as own a pair of underwear of any sort?

Like a child, he put on his socks with exaggerated care. He carried his boots, which he had found under the bed giving off an unfamiliar odor, in one hand. He slid his feet across the floor rather than step, so worried was he about making the slightest noise.

He tried to raise the window gently, but the wooden frame was stuck. Walt pushed harder and harder until the window finally flew up with a resounding bang that rattled plates in the parlor. Panicked, he jumped through the window head first instead of climbing. The windowsill hit him in the stomach and he hit his head on the porch. Somewhere in all the confusion, he had dropped his boots. One had landed inside the house and the other outside. He gathered them up hurriedly and rushed off towards his shack.

Walt arrived at his own door carrying his boots, his feet hurting from all the rocks he had stepped on along the way. Before going in, he stopped to put his boots on. This was the reverse of his usual routine. He normally took off his wet seaboots before coming inside, setting them just inside the door. This movement was unconscious to Walt, it was in fact instinctive to all Tristanian fishermen. To do the converse now was just a reflex action.

It was a reflex for which he was very grateful as soon as he opened the door. The vomit, which had lain so deep on the floor when he left, had not gone away of its own accord. The thickened puddles made it difficult for him to walk. He shuffled his way over to the trunk and took out a few of his possessions. These he placed carefully on the bed. He selected several favorites from his pile of sweaters and put them on his cot as well. He stuffed all these things into his small duffle bag and waded back to the door.

He had made up his mind. He was leaving Tristan.

VI

IN THE FIRST LIGHT OF DAWN he walked down to the beach, turned his boat right side up and pushed it across the sand to the water. He gave the boat a shove and jumped in. As soon as he had unshipped his oars and started rowing, he was on his way. It was as easy as that. Less than a week ago the possibility of leaving the island, even for a visit, had never even occurred to Walt. Now here he was leaving Tristan behind him.

It was as easy as that.

Well, actually, it was not quite as easy as that. In making his rather quick preparations for leaving the island, Walt had neglected to bring along food or water. Tristan, as you no doubt recall, is more than two thousand miles from any other landmass. It might seem apparent that this was not a well-prepared or provisioned journey.

Since oars were the little boat's only means of propulsion, Walt was compelled to look continually over the transom. He had no choice but to look back at Tristan all the while as he rowed away. Walt was not sentimental, but he became aware for perhaps the first time in his life of the enormity of the unknown.

For some reason he also felt no fear. Walt had spent his whole life in this small boat, but that was only in the waters immediately surrounding the island that was his home. He was aware of the dangers of the sea, but now felt no concern for them. His own survival had not occurred to him as an issue in getting ready to leave.

He had rowed for less than half an hour when the boat became caught in a strong current. Not seeing any reason in fighting, he let go of his oars and abandoned himself to the will of the sea.

At this point one might well consider Walt a goner. His chances for survival must seem very slim indeed.

After three or four hours at sea, just about the time Walt began to get his first real pangs of hunger and thirst, even he began to experience a dimming of his hopes.

Soon a squall blew up from the south. Walt's little boat was tossed by the sea. The rain began to fall. Here Walt made what was perhaps the best decision of his life. Deciding to sacrifice comfort for a better chance of survival, he took off his rubber boots.

He set them in the prow of the boat. By the time the rain cleared, after about an hour of heavy downpour, he had almost three inches of potable water in each boot. Walt realized that this would be enough water to keep him alive for at least a day. With the frequency of rainfall in this part of the ocean, he supposed that with some care he might well be able to catch enough water to keep him alive.

That left only the problem of food. This problem, too, solved itself in an unexpected manner. After some twelve hours at sea, when Walt was beginning to get very hungry indeed, a sixty pound Albacore tuna jumped into the boat, very nearly capsizing it.

Walt was surprised at having a creature so large suddenly decide to be his companion. He put out the oars to add stability to the tiny craft. He then pulled a rusty fishing knife from the bottom of the boat and stabbed the fish repeatedly until it stopped thrashing.

It never once crossed Walt's mind during this encounter that he might be manifesting incredibly bad manners by killing the only seagoing companion he had ever had. It also took a moment for him to realize that the fish, which he had thought of to that point only as an intruder, could also be a source of food.

Thus was established the pattern of Walt's life that would continue for the next five days. He kept his boots at all times ready to catch rainwater and sliced off a portion of the tuna whenever he became hungry. At night he lashed the oars in such a way that they acted as outriggers to give the boat more stability. He slept only fitfully.

In his survival, Walt felt for the first time in his life fortunate. He congratulated himself several times every day on his imagination in gathering water and in small things like tying knots. He had no vision for anything beyond surviving each day. He did not even get around to questioning his reasons for leaving the island, even though he had plenty of time to do so.

For practically any other human, those days alone at sea would have been torturous: drinking the fetid water from Walt's none-too-sanitary boots, eating slices from the decaying tuna, bits of rust from the knife embedding into each slice. The solitude alone would have tried the sanity of most.

Walt, however, was not like most people. He felt relieved by the solitude. For the first time in his memory, there was no one around to taunt him or make him feel uncomfortable. He felt no compulsion to hide or run from other people.

The diet was not so much different from what he had eaten on Tristan, except that the tuna was not cooked, of course. His piles of sweaters kept him reasonably warm. Most of all he enjoyed the sensation of spending all day alone on the water, where he had always felt most comfortable, without having to return to the Plant to drop off his catch. He realized that he had always hoped in some small way to sail off into the sunset, to leave Tristan far behind.

It is axiomatic that fishermen somehow long to be possessed by the sea. Walt had no way of explaining the slight disappointment he had always felt when he took his first step onto dry land after a day of fishing. He had now, in abandoning himself entirely to the ocean's will, actualized the symbiotic trust that fishermen have in the sea. He would endure because he was one with his boat and the water.

The reader will no doubt have noticed that the preceding bit of intellectualization came not from Walt, but from me. Forgive me if I intrude.

One other thing: Walt had no idea where he was or which way he was going. He had never had any occasion to go out of sight of land fishing for lobsters. As one might expect of the residents of the most isolated spot on Earth, Tristanians did not go about visiting other islands very often. Consequently, Walt knew absolutely nothing about navigation. He did not even know from what direction the sun rose, and into which it set. All he was aware of was the current that carried him along.

Walt was very fortunate to have strayed into this current, for it was reliably strong and steady. Important for Walt's future survival, it was also known to the captains of some ocean-going ships who used it to increase their speed and cut their fuel consumption.

It was for this reason, and this reason alone, that on the afternoon of Walt's seventh day at sea, he was spotted and picked up by the freighter *San Geronimo*.

Walt was of mixed feelings about being rescued. He knew that his precious solitude was at an end, and for this he was sorry. He also knew that the remains of the tuna would be totally inedible within one day. As it was, while on board the cargo ship, Walt would come down with a serious case of amoebic dysentery.

Walt's most pressing emotion as a skiff from the freighter was dispatched and drew near was one of incredible fear. He vaguely remembered from school on Tristan that people around the world spoke many different languages. Communicating was so difficult for him under any circumstances that he dreaded to think of what another language might be like.

One thing that bears mentioning before Walt is rescued: during his week at sea, Walt continued to hear the

Easybeats playing in his mind. The sound was in a way comforting to him. He now enjoyed its regularity and dependability. Along with the motion of the waves, the music was a constant in his life on his tiny vessel.

Another thing: even though Walt was only barely aware of it at the time, the music was already becoming louder and more distinct. If he thought about this phenomenon at all, and he would not have thought of it in such concrete terms, he probably attributed the increased strength of the signal to his familiarity with the music. If in fact that was what he thought, he was wrong.

In any case, the *San Geronimo's* tender soon drew near. As a heaving line was thrown, Walt had time for one last thought alone. He wondered if he would be received with the same revulsion that had been a constant part of his life on Tristan.

As it was, he was treated very warmly and civilly. He was brought aboard the freighter and his own little fishing skiff was hauled aboard and lashed to the deck. Walt was introduced to the Captain and given quarters to use until such a time as the freighter reached land or encountered authorities who could be of assistance to him.

In his bunk, Walt pondered the Captain's offer of assistance. For the first time he realized that, if he did not know what he was trying to accomplish, it was very unlikely for anyone to be able to help him achieve anything. He remembered that he had had an irresistible compulsion to leave the island and that this drive was somehow involved with the Easybeats. Riding along on the *San Geronimo* did not seem in any way contrary to his current mood, so he reasoned that it must be the appropriate thing to do.

He became even firmer in this reasoning when he considered his alternatives.

As has been previously mentioned, in the days following Walt's rescue by the freighter he was stricken with a severe case of dysentery. The ship's complement was too small to include a doctor, but the Second Mate had some interest in medicine. He treated Walt as best he could with the limited medical facilities aboard the ship. The Second Mate was a dedicated man and he cursed himself and his ship's provisioning when Walt did not respond to his treatment. The Second Mate was a kindly man and refrained from cursing Walt for failing to get better.

There was of course a reason why Walt was not getting better. The Second Mate had assumed that the source of Walt's intestinal parasites was the tuna. In fact, the microbes that now flourished in Walt's abdomen had originally come from his boots. They grew in the sun-warmed water of Walt's boots, which he used for drinking.

If the Second Mate had had access to a decent medical laboratory, he would have found that the organisms spawned in Walt's boots were of a completely unknown variety. Thus, Walt's disease was a truly new thing under the sun.

If this discovery had been made by the Second Mate, which it was not, several different things could have happened. He could have isolated the parasite, written a scientific paper about it, and been the man of the moment among the world's medical bacteriology community.

Not least among the pleasures of such an activity would have been the honor of naming the newly found organism. No one can say what he might have called the bacterium if he had discovered it. Perhaps he would have named it after Walt. Perhaps he would have named it after a certain woman in Singapore of whom he was fond, and visited without fail every time he sailed there.

Another thing: if he had capitalized on the discovery of this organism, a discovery which, I must repeat, he did not after all make, he could potentially have made a tremendous amount of money in the process. At that time, the Second Mate believed that he wanted to make a great deal of money, and that doing so would make him happy.

In what way could a sailor become wealthy from a microbe? There were at least fifteen governments around the world that would have paid dearly for a dysentery bacterium that bred in people's boots. They would pay even more when they found out that this particular organism was resistant to conventional antibiotic therapy.

There is of course a second possible outcome to this bacteria scenario. The organism could have run rampant through the crew, killing them all in one of the most unpleasant ways imaginable. Remember that the *San Geronimo* was still nearly two thousand miles from the nearest shore. She could have drifted for months, a ghost ship and a plague ship both, before being found by anyone.

It never crossed the Second Mate's mind that Walt might be carrying a disease which could eradicate all forms of life on the vessel, even the rats that lived in the deepest part of the hold.

But, again, the Second Mate never learned how drastically Walt's case of the trots could have changed the course of human history.

Walt, incidentally, recovered after not too long an illness. The Second Mate was reduced to explaining away Walt's recovery to his strong constitution and his willingness to undertake bed rest.

Quite honestly, the Second Mate had absolutely no idea what had in fact cured Walt. Walt had very wisely chosen to tell no one aboard the ship about the music in his head. Thus the Second Mate had no reason to test Walt's electromagnetic field. As it was there was no test equipment available aboard the vessel that could detect the field that Walt emanated, a field which was slowly but steadily increasing in power.

The microbes had flourished for a time in Walt's magnetic field. In fact, the reason that Walt's complaint was not contagious was simply that no one else on the ship, or on the face of the Earth, had a similar electromagnetic resonance. As the amplitude of the field increased, Walt's intestines became an increasingly hostile environment for the parasites. When the oscillatory amplitude became critical, the microbes simply exploded.

One other thing: Walt's powerful magnetic field was also subtly throwing off the accuracy of the ship's navigational equipment. The members of the crew had no way of detecting it, but the *San Geronimo* was already drifting off course.

Walt, who considered his whole life to revolve around boats and the sea, had in fact never been aboard a vessel more than four meters in length. With the exception of one, every boat he had ever seen had been powered by the wind or oars. The sole exception was an ancient five horsepower outboard motor that belonged to a second cousin of his.

Under such circumstances, one might assume that a seaman would be interested in touring a modern vessel. Walt, however, had no interest in the propulsion, cargo, navigation, or bridge sections of the ship. The only parts that held his interest were the galley and, far more strongly, his own bunk.

This was not due entirely to his fear of the members of the crew. Everyone on board the ship had been very nice to him. Apparently they expected a castaway to be decrepit in appearance and solitary in manner. Even the Captain had several times come to Walt's bunk to ask if he was receiving satisfactory treatment from the Second Mate, who seemed be the only member of the crew with whom Walt had any regular contact.

Walt always responded that he was being treated very well on board the ship, he just had no interest in being anywhere but his bunk just then. He thanked the Captain, or whoever might be addressing him at the moment, for visiting, then rolled over and went to sleep, or merely rested.

Incidentally, there is one fact which has not been mentioned about Walt's physical condition. When the Second Mate examined him, it was discovered that Walt had chlamydia. The Second Mate felt that this was not a matter to be discussed, and so did not tell Walt about his condition.

This oversight no doubt saved both Walt and the Second Mate a great deal of confusion and embarrassment. The Second Mate was saved from having to broach a difficult and personal subject. He also avoided having to explain to Walt about the nature of such diseases and how they are transmitted.

If Walt had been able to grasp the concepts involved in such a diagnosis, he would have been shocked. Walt firmly believed that he was a virgin. His one kiss with Leonore had been, so far as he knew, his most intimate contact with another member of his species.

Walt, of course, had no memory of the time that he was unconscious at the Wilkins' residence. After he had collapsed, Mrs. Wilkins had called Leonore out of hiding to assist her in getting Walt to bed. Their motives had been, to begin with, entirely chaste.

Putting him to bed, they discovered what many had long suspected: a man's center of sexual response is in no way connected to his processors of conscious and rational thought. For the three days he remained unconscious, he was limp in every part of his body save one.

Mrs. Wilkins and Leonore both were enchanted by the idea of a man who never interrupted them or distracted them from the things that they wanted to do, yet was continually ready to be used by them to satisfy their pleasures. They both threw themselves on him repeatedly, together and separately, in every combination and permutation their long-dormant drives could imagine.

Leonore had in fact finished with him just minutes before he awoke. Feeling Walt beginning to stir underneath her, she climbed off and ran upstairs as quickly as she could, yelling a warning to her mother as she rounded a corner.

Walt had of course been put to bed in Leonore's bedroom, where every scrap of clothing she owned was kept. She was thus forced to hide upstairs entirely naked until Walt left the house. As may be recalled, this did not occur until many hours later when he made his clamorous dive out the window.

As it was, Walt would never find out that Leonore had been anywhere but at her Aunt's house mending clothes. He would also never know whether any of those encounters had resulted in offspring. As it turns out, Mrs. Wilkins was pregnant with twins by Walt. Leonore was in fact sterile because she had suffered for years from an untreated case of chlamydia which she had caught from a philatelic collector of fanatical devotion who was visiting Tristan on vacation.

In any case, chlamydia was one complaint which did respond exactly as expected to antibiotic treatment. In no time at all, Walt was completely healed, without even having had the luxury of knowing the nature of his complaint.

Walt floated through his days on a sea of unawareness. There were so many things he did not know about his life; things he did not even bother to ask about. He spent afternoons in his bunk, blissfully ignorant of his surroundings.

Now, for the first time, he found himself actually listening to the Easybeats, who were continuing the endless repetition of their greatest hit inside his head. For the first time, he begen to wonder just what exactly was meant by the lyrics. He surprised himself by thinking about the music and how the different parts went together. In all, he found that he enjoyed the companionship of the music.

One night, when Walt was almost completely recovered from his bout with dysentery, an odd thing happened. For the first time in living memory he had a dream. He dreamt that he got out of his bunk. So realistic was the dream that he could feel the cold steel decking under his bare feet. He climbed the ladder leading to the main deck, wrapping his toes around the rungs for purchase.

As he walked across the deck in his dream, he felt the cold wind billowing out the pajamas that one of the sailors had given him. He climbed into the tower, the nerve center of the ship.

He saw that he was in a room filled with pictures and strange tools. He had never seen anything the least like any of the things in that room. Somehow he felt like he knew what he was doing.

He grabbed one of the pictures and started drawing. He drew lines and circles in black and in several other colors. Finally, he knew he was done.

At that moment, just as one might suspect, the lights snapped on. The sailor standing watch at that point came in to see what Walt was doing in the navigation room. The Captain was summoned.

Walt stood shivering in his ridiculous sleeping clothes. He blinked his eyes, having trouble adjusting to the light.

At last the Captain appeared, dressed in his own pair of

rather ridiculous seeming pajamas. He asked Walt what he thought he was doing in a part of the ship, the only part of the ship in fact, in which he was not welcome without one of the crew.

Walt was only barely able to explain that he did not think he was there; that is, he thought he was dreaming when he went there. He fought his embarrassment, trying as hard as he possibly could to get across to these people, these strangers, that he had not done any of this on purpose. Finally he broke into continual apologies. He apologized several times to every person in the room. He apologized to most of the equipment in the room. He apologized to the ship.

The Captain tired of hearing Walt's apologies. He glanced around the small room. His eyes landed on unfamiliar markings on the chart. He let out an exclamation as he saw what Walt had done.

Walt had computed a great circle course that took maximum advantage of prevailing winds and currents. Walt's calculations even took into consideration the tidal effects of the phases of the moon.

It was, in short, a brilliant piece of navigation. If Nobel Prizes or Pulitzer Prizes or Academy Awards were available in navigation, Walt's course would have swept all of them. It was the finest piece of work the Captain had ever seen. The Captain immediately tried to hire Walt on as the ship's navigator, but Walt kept insisting that he had no idea what he had done. Among Walt's many apologies was one that intrigued the Captain. Walt said that he had not done any of this at all, the Easybeats had done it for him.

The Captain ordered that Walt's course be strictly followed from that moment on. He did not want to lose any of the advantages of the current moon phase, or other obscure factors which he may have missed in studying Walt's course.

Perhaps one very important detail has been omitted from all this talk about navigation. That detail is, of course, where the course finally wound up.

Walt's plotted trajectory for the ship intersected with land thirteen minutes south of the Thirty-Eighth Parallel. By Walt's calculations, within ten days the *San Geronimo* would arrive in San Francisco.

It may seem odd that the Captain acceded so easily to following Walt's course. The reason for this was simple: the *San Geronimo* was bound for San Francisco anyway. Walt's course would just bring them to their destination much faster and more efficiently.

As Walt was escorted back to his bunk, the music in his head became louder than ever.

VII

A T THIS POINT I FIND MYSELF compelled to break into the flow of the narrative again. Since Walt is now approaching my home, and our inevitable meeting, I feel I should make some things clear.

As probably everyone has guessed by now, the transmitter I had built on top of my apartment building was playing the Easybeats twenty-four hours a day. Walt was receiving the signal from my transmitter on his fillings. The amalgam of silver and mercury used in dental fillings can make a fine radio antenna if one has the right head shape, and is exposed to the proper frequencies.

I submit here that I built the transmission unit without any thought or indication that it might one day bring a lobster fisherman to my door. I had actually built the thing in an attempt to communicate with other planets.

I had felt for some time that the reason beings from other worlds never responded to official attempts at communication was that the government always sent such stupid, boring messages. I felt the need to send a message that would be bound to attract aliens actually interested in the commonalities of culture. I felt that any race sufficiently advanced to receive messages from another world would not really be interested in an endless loop of the first hundred-thousand digits of pi. That could only be old news, a clutter of the interplanetary void. No, music, I was certain, would make for much more interesting communication.

I had long noticed the difficulty humans have in resisting good music, and had hoped that such a trait might be universal. My plan then was simple: beam a great song out into space as an invitation and wait to see who stopped by.

I submit here also that of all the creatures I imagined responding to my hail, I never dreamt of one even remotely as strange as Walt.

VIII

IN ANY CASE, THE REMAINDER of Walt's journey was relatively uneventful. The members of the crew shied away from him whenever possible. Sailors are suspicious and superstitious people, and this batch was very uncomfortable with having a suddenly prodigious navigator in their midst.

Some of the crewmen thought he had been possessed. Others thought he was an agent of a foreign government, or an agent of their own shipping line sent to test them. One or two thought he might be an eccentric genius millionaire from the electronics industry who was larking on some sort of a thrill vacation.

All of the crew felt that he was not to be trusted. The Captain stopped visiting him. Even the Second Mate grew distant and cold.

Walt told himself that he did not mind. He tried to enjoy the solitude as he had in his own boat, but found that the pleasure was not forthcoming. He felt that he had been close to acceptance with these sailors; they had treated him better than anyone had ever treated him before. Now he felt a failure. Something that he had done, something he had done while he was asleep, had driven all of them away from him.

He also realized that it is possible to be somehow less alone in a small boat with no one else aboard than it is to be among others, but ignored, in a larger boat. This was a tremendously urbane lesson for any Tristanian to appreciate. Many, many people only truly appreciate this aloneness when they have left the comfort of their family and friends for the unknown excitements of a large city. Walt, of course, had left the routine and friendless discomforts of his island home for an unknown future away from Tristan.

But Walt was not entirely alone. Even when everyone else failed him, he still had the Easybeats in his head to keep him company.

Incidentally, by this time the Easybeats had taken up residence in San Francisco. They moved into the boiler room in the basement of a building on Tehama Alley, which they were able to rent very cheaply due to an enormous population of rats reluctant to share their home. The apartment, if it can be called that, was less than three blocks from my own.

They also got a job working as the night manager of the twenty-four hour pool hall underneath the Denny's restaurant in Japantown. It might appear to an insightful observer that the Easybeats preferred to be underground.

At this time, I had no idea that the band playing on my transmitter were my new neighbors. Of course, I had no idea of Walt's existence, either.

I spent my time much as I always had; thinking, walking around the city, playing the meager extent of my piano repertoire, drinking coffee, even writing occasionally. My roommate was off trekking somewhere in Asia, so I did not anticipate having company any time in the near future. I was soon to find out that I was wrong in that presumption.

All that, of course, will be told when the proper time has come.

Meanwhile, Walt and the others steamed steadily and highly efficiently towards San Francisco.

The Captain of the *San Geronimo* had by now turned over most of the duties of running the ship to his First and Second Mates. The Captain himself remained locked in the ship's chart room studying Walt's course. From days of scrutiny, the Captain was able to determine that such a course could only have been laid with knowledge of long-term trends in the Earth's hydrologic and gravitational cycles. The Captain was no dummy. He was also intrigued by the fact that the course took them on an arc of the Earth's surface, a Great Circle, rather than a straight linear path. He knew that such trajectories only made sense if the navigator were able to see, or imagine, the territory from above.

He was never able to deduce how Walt was able to figure this course, but, then, that had never in itself been his main intention. He was interested in reproducing Walt's results. He knew that if he did, it would form the basis of a great revolution in navigation. He imagined, quite rightly, that such knowledge could make him an enormously wealthy man. The Captain, much like his Second Mate, felt that he genuinely wanted money and that having a great deal of it would make him very happy indeed.

As it was, he never succeeded in uncovering all the secrets of the course that had been unveiled to him. However, the bonus that the shipping company paid him for the time and fuel saved on the voyage was enough for him to start a modest fleet of his own, which he did. Through years of study and experimentation he was able to start a revolution in navigation culminating in his founding a company which made shipboard computers to assist in the tremendously complicated calculations necessary for even the simplest forms of the new method.

This company made him richer than he had ever thought to dream. Within fifteen years he owned more vessels than any person or military organization on the planet. Within twenty years, he owned eighty-five percent of all the ships on the seas. Twenty-two years, seven months and six days after Walt had drawn his fateful diagram, the Captain, then called by many the Admiral, died a horrible death in an accident so repugnant and unlikely that there was a great deal of speculation to the effect that it seemed to have been some twenty years in the planning.

In all his years of work and study he never did quite match the accuracy of Walt's calculations, even though he had banks of computers and technical assistants helping him twenty-four hours each day. And Walt had done it without the aid of even a single scrap of scratch paper.

The problem he faced was this: the course that his calculations came up with was invariably off by a factor of up to one and seven sixteenths degrees. Over a course of hundreds or thousands of miles, this cumulative error could be quite substantial. Nonetheless, navigation by the Captain's approximate method was such an advantage over conventional means of course-plotting that most navigators took to using the new techniques to get the ship roughly to where it was supposed to go, and then switching back to the traditional methods to bring themselves into port.

Some years after the Captain's death, a Japanese physicist named Bruno von Gottlieb proved that the deflection was precisely equal to that which would be caused by an electromagnetic field of such strength that it could actually cause a slight warping in the localized gravity field. In the case of the *San Geronimo*, this field, in von Gottlieb's hypothesis, would be centered at the precise location of Walt's bunk.

Walt, of course, would never know any of this.

IX

A T LONG LAST THE *SAN GERONIMO* arrived in San
Francisco. Walt found his familiar shipboard routine
suddenly at an end. He was assaulted by the presence of a
modern city. An average residential block in San Francisco
contains many times as many inhabitants as the entire
island of Tristan de Cunha. Walt had no idea that such a
population of humans existed as he saw in his first moment off the ship's gangplank.

The sailors all had business to attend to ashore. They
forgot about Walt in their hurry to do things and find
things and sell things. Within minutes Walt found himself alone on the pier. Without noticing it, he had begun
to sing along with the music in his head.

I had spent the last several hours riding the N Judah
back and forth again. At the end of the line, Embarcadero
Station, I decided to get off the train and stretch my legs
for a while.

I walked down to the foot of Market Street, past the
Vallaincourt Fountain and under the broken-off stubs of
the Embarcadero Freeway. I turned right, walking towards
the working docks instead of the hopeless tourist installa-

tions to the left.

I had not gone very far when I saw what could have been a male human. He was shuffling around, looking very lost indeed, and quite frightened too. San Francisco has a large population of homeless people, many of whom have severe mental health problems. It is a daily event to see these people wandering around. They are a fact of life in this city.

Two things about this person, however, attracted my attention. These are the reasons: first, he did not look at all like a street person. He was wearing several wool sweaters and knee-high rubber fisherman's boots. He did not seem to be suffering from the privations that the homeless endure daily. Second, he was singing the Easy-beats.

I do not really know why, perhaps I felt responsible somehow, but I approached this man. I spoke to him in the calmest words I could muster. I asked him his name, he said he was Walt.

There, it is done. Walt and I have met.

X

OUR CONVERSATION LASTED far longer than it reasonably should have. I finally worked in a question about his interest in the Easybeats. Cryptically, and at great length, he described to me the nature of his ordeal. That information makes up the bulk of the preceding pages of this story.

I asked him how long he had been hearing the music in his head. As I have said before, I was not prepared for creatures quite as strange as Walt to answer my beacon. At that point I did not tell him that I was, in all likelihood, transmitting the signal that he had heard in his head all this time.

I took Walt down the street to Red's Java House for coffee. I hoped that it would be something of a familiar environment for him. Red's is built out over the water on piers. The drain from the sink goes through a hole in the floor and directly out into the Bay.

The crowd there is mostly longshoremen and visiting sailors, but a lot of frugal suits from the Financial District come there for the coffee and the cheap hamburgers that taste like vinegar. The walls are covered with posters announcing union meetings and other types of workingmen's information.

Walt was in a state of shock. The coffee did not seem to help. I had no idea that he had never tasted coffee before.

Our conversation finally got around to his plans here. His response was simple: he had none. His response was exactly the same when I asked him about his place to stay. What I did next seemed logical enough at the time, but has never made sense to me since; I invited him to come stay with me.

After all, he was not really going to be in the way. My roommate had contracted Dengue Fever while traveling across northern Thailand by elephant and, after a period of bed rest in Delhi, had traveled to Salt Lake City to recuperate.

I did not think at that point to ask how long Walt might be planning on staying with me. As things turned out, it did not really matter.

After finishing our coffee, we walked up Folsom all the way from the waterfront to get back to my, our, apartment. Walt was terrified by the enormity of the Bay Bridge and the buildings downtown. I had a great deal of difficulty describing the purpose of Alcatraz before it became a tourist attraction. There were, of course, no prisons on Tristan.

Walt told me that the music in his head was getting louder and louder with every step. Conversation became progressively more difficult. By the time we crossed Fifth Street, I had to shout to make myself heard over the din in Walt's head. I made a mental note to bring down the power on the transmitter.

As we walked on in silence I wondered what could possibly have caused my transmission in San Francisco to be picked up in the head of a lobster fisherman half way around the world.

I finally hit upon a theory. I remembered that certain radio frequencies are subject to a phenomenon known as "wave skip". When this happens, the radio wave is reflected off of the Earth's atmosphere and sent back down to the surface of the planet. If the angles all line up just perfectly, the signal can be carried thousands, even tens of thousands, of miles beyond the normal transmitting range of the radio source. This skip is most common with relatively low frequency radio waves. I had opted for a low frequency transmitter because I thought it would be more difficult for the Government to trace. The Government has some draconian ideas about the nature of broadcasting and who should be allowed to be involved in it. I was actually breaking the law by transmitting my innocent message to the stars. Laws, I have found, are by and large foolish inventions.

I was a bit saddened by the idea of the skipping waves. If the theory was correct, it meant that my signal had not penetrated the atmosphere at all. No creature in space could have heard my transmission, or so I then thought.

But at least it had brought me Walt. I supposed that my experiment was a success then. A being had picked up my signal and honed in on it, finally making contact with me.

The only question that remained was how Walt had

been receiving my signal all this time. He did not seem to have any obvious antennae or anything like that. I shouted a question to him: did he have any dental work?

He proudly showed me a mouth full of fillings, caps, bridges, and unremoved bits of braces. A number of years before, an ambitious young Tristanian had undertaken a correspondence course in dentistry, since the island had no dentist.

Tristanians traditionally have excellent teeth, thus allowing their group to survive quite peacefully for generations without dental care, but, in this case, the twentieth century was not to be eluded. The young man, whose name was Brian, was determined to be a dentist.

Brian studied hard and made rapid progress in his course. He had only one problem. He found it extremely difficult to find real patients on whom to practice. Most of the island's population were repulsed by the idea of the young man drilling into their teeth or doing other such things. Even those few farsighted individuals who thought it a good idea to have a trained dentist on the island refused to visit Brian professionally until he had received his diploma. Unfortunately for Brian, he needed to perform a certain amount of real dental work before he could officially graduate from his program.

Enter Walt. Although this time it had never been officially acknowledged, Walt had saved Brian from drowning just as surely as he had the overboard fisherman, and just as inadvertently.

Walt was excited when he first heard that Brian would perform free dental work on any volunteer who would agree to come forward before his dental degree was finalized.

On Walt's first visit, Brian was disappointed to see that Walt did not require anything more than a cleaning. Not wanting to foul up his first opportunity to work on a real patient, though, Brian put three or four fillings in Walt's teeth.

In another related paradox of Brian's dental education, he could not sign a prescription for any anesthetics until he was certified as a dentist. Even after his graduation, if it ever came, it might take months for the first shipment of Novocain and laughing gas to reach the island. Brian believed that word of this lack of vital medication had spread around the island, thus diminishing even further his chances of attracting patients.

Walt never seemed to mind the lack of painkillers. Years later, as Brian became the elder statesman of Tristanian dentistry, he would recall that he never had a patient as stoic as Walt, and his paying customers, after the degree finally came, had all been safely medicated.

Brian discovered something else about dentistry that first day, the first time he put a drill to Walt's teeth. It was not discussed in his illustrated dental textbooks, and was not a feature of the otherwise realistic dental dummies and models of teeth that were sent with each lesson. That very first time, Brian drilled far too far into Walt's tooth and discovered blood.

Walt was not to be dissuaded. He returned to Brian weekly for checkups. That is twenty-six times more often than even the most scrupulous hygienists recommend dental visits. To put it another way, he received 2,600% of the dental care required to keep his teeth in top shape.

At every visit, Brian undertook some unneeded repair to Walt's mouth. Walt now did not have a single tooth in his mouth that had not been filled or filed or capped or crowned or canalled in the roots or linked with its neighbors by elaborate systems of metal ropes and pulleys. Brian probably would have pulled all of Walt's teeth for the experience of making dentures, but knew that to do so would be to destroy a wonderful thing. He knew that he could not justify, even to Walt, the necessity of performing elaborate oral surgery on false teeth. After all, if he wanted to do that, Walt could just leave the appropriate plate at Brian's house, where all the work was done, before he went out on his boat in the morning. No, Walt needed his real teeth to continue being Brian's walking one-man laboratory.

In any case, it should be apparent enough by now that Walt had enough antenna material in his mouth to rival Sutro Tower. The signals were picked up on the dental work and resonated through his perfectly-shaped head which rang with only the frequency from my transmitter.

I was struck by a feeling for which I had no name. I had horribly disrupted this man's life, brought him from his home. Well, I rationalized, people came to San Francisco from all over the world for many stupid reasons. Walt at least seemed to be here on some sort of a mission.

XI

WALKING BACK UP HOWARD STREET I decided that
we should stop in at the Seventh Street Senior
Social Center. Normally, absolutely no one under age 65
is allowed in the doors, but I know the doormen, Säid and
Arvin. Once in a while they let me in to observe.

There is an elaborate myth that the Center is some sort
of club. The exclusive age rule conveniently keeps snoop-
ers and tourists, and for the most part the police, away.

The Center, after all, is not what it appears to be. Pub-
licly they are known for the senior nutrition programs and
meager entertainments that are advertised or sometimes
reported in the more charitable media.

The Center is located at Sixth and Howard, the epi-
center of San Francisco's skid row. Almost invisible in the
masses of poor and drunks and diseased of all varieties are
the huge numbers of indigent elderly. Before the Center
opened its doors, these people were only occasionally seen
shuffling around being easy victims on the days the Social
Security checks came out; or perhaps in the corner store
buying the cheapest forms of human sustenance available,
occasionally with some slight attempt at spiritual rein-

forcement through a tiny flask of brandy.

In the eighteen months since the opening of the Center, the community had been transformed. Hundreds of old, really old, and beyond ancients lined the sidewalk each morning, waiting for the doors to open at noon.

For the admission price of two dollars, each person would be fed and allowed to stay for the duration of the afternoon. Lunch was always the same. Every retiree paying the two-dollar fee received a bowl of mashed potatoes with hamburger gravy and a bowl of creamed corn. The meal came with a spoon and a paper napkin.

The real action began after everyone had eaten. The doors were locked, latecomers be damned. The Center transformed itself into a gambling hall.

It surprised me, as it must have surprised everyone, with the possible exception of the owners, how much money these supposedly indigent old farts could come up with. Nearly every penny of their social security, retirement, and the last of their savings were withered away on keno and bingo and roulette.

The most popular game was, as far as I know, unique to the center. It carried the added attraction of being absolutely free to play. This was the Sleeping Pit.

The Pit itself was a round sunken affair, somewhat like a hot tub, but about three times as large. It was lined in soft green felt. A bench ran around the edge of the circle. The seat was made of a strange material which was just soft enough to conform to the shape of the person sitting, yet firm enough to provide comfortable support to the most arthritic pensioner for hours on end.

The game was simple. The first twenty-five customers to sign up after lunch were gently escorted into the Pit. Able-bodied young assistants were employed to make sure that the players were not injured on the inbound climb.

Once all the contestants were comfortably seated, the clock was started. The rules of the game were amazingly simple: the clock would run for one hour. Anyone in the Pit still awake at the end of the hour would win $1,000.00 in cash. This game had been played every day, including Sundays, for a year and a half now. In all that time, not one person had been able to stay awake for more than twelve minutes.

The old people were obsessed with the game. No one could figure out why those in the pit fell asleep while the rest of the patrons, playing bingo, say, remained awake and active. It just did not make sense.

Failing to see any reason for the continual losses, every single patron felt that all the others were weak willed and that he or she alone could win. Remarkably, regular customers still felt this was the case even after they themselves had fallen asleep ten or fifteen times in the Pit. The financial motivation was great, too. A thousand dollars would enable any of them to be able to pay the move-in costs for a real apartment that they could afford on their monthly checks instead of the horrible hotels in which they now resided.

And so, every single day, hundreds awaited their chance to be humiliated by the Pit. Fights occasionally broke out over disputes as to who had signed up when. Old people who had relied on each other for survival since arriving at some Sixth Street flophouse now elbowed each other sharply in the ribs and swung handbags violently in the mad rush to sign up.

By the time Walt and I arrived, the day's contestants had been in the Pit for five minutes or so. Säid led us down an alley. A door opened onto a passage leading to the Center's office. The office was equipped with two way mirrors and elaborate video equipment, which gave multiple views of the Pit area.

More than half the contestants were asleep already. Walt watched in fascination. I did not realize at the time that he had never seen a television before. He also had no knowledge of two-way mirrors. The concept was very difficult to explain.

Having to explain to Walt what was going on lessened my ability to concentrate on what was happening inside the room. I always enjoyed watching the suckers fall asleep. They yawned. They stretched. Their mouths fell open. Many of them drooled. I could see the lines of care and worry evaporating from their faces. Many of them looked years younger. They all seemed to find a release, a kind of total sleep, a resting of the parts of the mind which were usually occupied with dreams and memories. I had suspected for some time that it was this escapist sleep as much as the lure of the money which brought in the crowds.

In another five minutes or so, all the old people were fast asleep. They would remain that way for the duration of the hour. For some reason, Walt looked disturbed. We went out into the alley, which connected Howard Street with Folsom Street, and continued walking.

XII

WE AT LAST REACHED my apartment. Walt seemed to enjoy its comfortable smallness. I suppose it might have reminded him of a snug Tristanian home, or perhaps a boat of some sort.

He did not comment on the interior decoration. I thought this odd until I realized that he had no idea of what was the normal method of livening up one's home with things in this part of the world.

My roommate was a great collector of lunchboxes. Lunchboxes lined every wall from floor to ceiling, hundreds of them. It was not uncommon for him, the roommate, to spend thousands of dollars at a time for particularly rare or beautiful boxes. Walt must have considered this normal decor. Perhaps it was just the first of any number of misconceptions which I fed him.

There was, of course, my piano to contend with as well. I was a little surprised to learn that, in the midst of Walt's worldly inexperience, mine was not the first grand piano he had seen. Of the few visitors who have come to my small apartment, most have been intimidated by my piano. To reach any part of the small studio save the bathroom, it is necessary to climb either over or under the piano. It also doubles as my tabletop, writing surface, and ladder for climbing to my bed, which lives up on stilts to preserve precious floor space. Walt was different. He seemed to genuinely enjoy the piano, and admire its multitude of uses.

Walt was now visibly in pain from the intensity of the transmitter. After all, I had built the thing to communicate with another planet, and it had a power supply several dozens of times as strong as the Federal Communications Commission would have allowed. I found myself faced with a real problem. How could I get away from Walt, who was by now following me like a puppy, for long enough to get up on the roof and modulate transformer power? And, if I could even do this much, how could I avoid blowing my cover?

I hit on a plan that was remarkably simple. I was able to get across to Walt with shouting and some impromptu sign language that my roommate, the owner of the lunchboxes, had magical powers. Through living with him, I had been able to slowly become initiated into some of the mysterious powers which my roomie possessed.

I told Walt that each of the lunchboxes helped protect the bearer from a different form of evil or sickness. I told him that children most often carried them because their parents wanted to protect them from harm.

I selected one of my favorite boxes, a red "Bullwinkle", and rummaged around for some string. I told Walt that I would have to perform some very involved incantations alone and outdoors. I explained to him that the roof of the apartment building was the ideal place for this. However, the magic of the charm would work only if Walt received the box without my coming back inside. Of course it could only protect him as long as he kept it in his immediate physical presence.

Walt seemed to buy the story. Stuffing some basic tools into my pockets, and telling Walt to open the window and wait, I headed up towards the roof.

I spun about twenty feet of twine off of the spool and bit through it. I wedged a screwdriver into the main rheostat of the transmitter's power amplifier and tied the length of twine to the handle. I carried the loose end of the string with me to the edge of the building.

After waiting what seemed a sufficient amount of time for incantations to have taken place, I tied the handle of the lunchbox to the twine still on the spool. Calling out for Walt, I started lowering the lunchbox to the window of the apartment.

I saw Walt lean out the window. Just as his fingers grazed the lunchbox, I pulled on the string tied to the screwdriver. Miraculously the whole contraption managed to work. Walt caught the lunchbox just as I had the power down to a level where he could still hear the Easybeats clearly but without pain.

Neither Walt nor I knew it at the time, but just a few blocks away, the Easybeats got very nervous. The Easybeats are well known in certain circles for being impatient and edgy. When the power went down on my transmitter, they literally jumped several feet into the air, hitting their heads on a low beam in the ceiling of their boiler room home.

When I had returned to my apartment I found Walt greatly relieved. He looked as I have imagined Hercules must have when he tricked Atlas into holding the world again.

XIII

IT IS DIFFICULT FOR ME TO DESCRIBE the days following, during which Walt and I were constant companions. I showed him the City and, little bits at a time, exposed him to life as I lived it. We rode the bus to Golden Gate Park to look at the buffalo. We ate adzuki bean ice cream, in a dish with a cone on the side, at Joe's Ice Cream down on Geary, the street on which I was born. We walked for hours on end, spent whole days sometimes in the museums, particularly the Museum of Modern Art. Walt was fascinated by the paintings, pictures like he had never imagined on Tristan. He completely surprised me during one of our trips by announcing that he might, someday, like to try his hand at painting.

We were, both of us, experiencing friendship for the first time. I found Walt childlike in that he had so little understanding of things that I took for granted. Yet with Walt I found none of the distance I had always felt around children. Walt I could talk to.

Somewhere along the line he had taken to continually humming the music that made counterpoint to whatever was going on around him. The music of the Easybeats was with us wherever we went on those days.

One adventure particularly sticks in my mind. We had by this time explored most of what I felt we could see on reasonable walks and bus rides. Walt had never ridden in a car. It was time for the 49 Mile Drive.

The 49 Mile Scenic Drive was created by the City as a means of low-cost automotive entertainment for tourists. It is supposed to take half a day and cover most of the major points of interest to those visiting San Francisco. That is the official version.

There is an old joke here that no native San Franciscan has ever actually completed the Drive. I have proven this wrong innumerable times. The rhythms of the Drive are familiar to me. I know all the difficult spots where the path is not well marked. I know the way through the park, and I know which way to go at Webster Street.

To me the drive is something philosophical. It is the closest thing I have to a religion. It makes for a wonderful panorama of misunderstanding. Places are passed by before there is any possibility of exploring or understanding. Like life, I suppose, the Drive covers a great deal of ground in less than a day.

In any case, the Drive requires a car, and that is one item which I did not have. I knew that it would not be much of a problem; it would simply require a visit to Jose, King of the Parking Lot.

Walt and I walked up to Nob Hill carrying packages of food and small things that we thought we might be of use during the Drive. Walt, of course had his constant companion lunchbox held closely by his side. I had by this time told him that lunchboxes were also useful for carrying things, especially food. Pandering to Walt's fascination with the thermos, I had made some hot soup for him.

He was trying to drink some out of the red plastic cup as we walked up the hill. His attempts were unsuccessful; he was splashing it all over himself. I was thinking ahead to the Drive and not talking. The only sound aside from the shuffling of our feet was Walt slurping his soup and occasionally letting out little yelps when he spilled some and burned himself.

Just over the crest of the hill, barely out of the shadow of Grace Cathedral, is the parking garage over which Jose presides. Whenever I arrive at the garage, Jose is invariably found sitting on the floor in a full lotus position, eyes closed. His breathing is impossibly slow and controlled. One side of his head is substantially larger than the other, swollen upward in a strange way.

Perhaps I should note before the narrative proceeds any further that the garage which I currently describe is located in one of the wealthiest quarters of the City. Rich people pay huge sums of money to rent reserved spaces in Jose's garage. In so doing, they ensure that they will never have to deal with the problems of parking and tickets and towing that make up such a large part of life for other local drivers.

Many of Jose's patrons have three or four or more vehicles living in the garage. Since the number of vehicles they can be using at any one time is limited, I figure that they will never notice if I should happen to use one of their cars for an afternoon. I have a routine which has never failed me.

I walk up to Jose and nudge him with my knee. This seldom rouses him from his meditation so I grab him by the shoulder and shake. When his eyes finally open, I yell at him and abuse him as I imagine his rich customers must. Jose has a terrible memory, or so it seems. He always seems to recognize me, but is never sure if I am a customer or something else.

At this point I call him an ingrate and an incompetent. I announce that I will take all my vehicles out of the garage if he does not produce my favorite car immediately. Whichever car he brings around I am grateful for. I smile at him and tip him generously for his efforts. As I drive away, I can see out the mirror that he has already crossed his legs and is again farther away from the San Francisco I can see than Walt ever was on Tristan.

It was in precisely this manner which I obtained a car for Walt and I to use on the Drive.

Jose disappeared into the recesses of the garage, seeming more to float than walk. I have never been a great fancier of cars, but I have always enjoyed the tension and the expectation that rises whenever Jose disappears into the nether recesses of his domain to bring out a car for me to use.

As he rounded the corner from wherever in his concrete dungeon the car had been parked, I studied his expression behind the wheel. It was ethereal. He seemed to be on the receiving end of some sort of cosmic bliss that may or may not have been connected to the car. My guess is that it probably was not.

It took me a while before I thought to look at the car. It was white and sort of boxy looking. It was not any kind that I had seen before, or that really grabbed my attention. I did notice that it was a convertible. The tan colored top was up.

Only when Jose had pulled up right in front of me did I recognize the insignia on the grill. Jose left the car idling when he got out. He left the driver's side door open, and ran around to open the other door for Walt. Walt eagerly climbed into the car, but I stood by the open door blankly staring at the pedals.

Jose had brought me a Ferrari.

I was worried for several reasons. One, of course, was that joyriding a car worth as much as a whole block of homes in the Sunset District was probably a very serious offense. This risk I could accept. The problem I was staring at was the mysterious third pedal on the left. I had never driven a stick shift before.

I very nearly lost my control at that point. I was worried that Jose might discover my fraud. I looked over at him, but he was already sitting on the concrete floor in a full lotus position, his head back in the stars.

I climbed into the car.

I tried to do everything very slowly, with much thought in every action. I knew you used the clutch every time you wanted to switch between gears. At least, I thought, I have a good theoretical understanding of what I will be doing. I had also noticed that people with stick-shift cars used their emergency brake much more frequently than was the norm in cars equipped with automatic transmissions.

My first thought, then, was to locate the brake handle in the Ferrari. It was off to my left, between the edge of the seat and the door. The handle was all the way down. I thought that perhaps Jose had forgotten to set the brake. That seemed to make enough sense.

By this time Walt was staring at me curiously. Even though it was his first time in a car, he seemed to have some suspicion that everything was not quite in order.

Breaking any sort of eye contact with him, I put the clutch pedal all the way to the floor, moved the shifting handle into the slot marked with a one and gently stepped on the gas.

The engine made a racing, whirring sound. I realized that I probably should take my foot off the clutch. When I did this, the tone of the engine changed to a much deeper roar. We still were not moving.

In a blast of insight I grabbed for the emergency brake lever. I pulled up on it and noticed that it did not make any clicking noise. I pulled further until it felt like I had caught hold of something. Then I pressed the button and felt a tremendous surge as I let the handle down.

By this time the car was making a great deal of noise, but we were hardly moving. I stepped on the gas even harder. The car felt as if it were ice skating, gently moving forward as it wobbled from side to side. The horrible smell of burning rubber filled the garage, and in the mirror I could see blue smoke pouring out from the back wheels. Through the rapidly thickening cloud of smoke I saw Jose open one eye.

Just then, fortunately, oh fortunately, the wheels got a grip on the pavement and we were gone. We shot out onto Sacramento Street. Just a few car lengths ahead of us was the stop sign. I jammed on the brake and the clutch, actually managing to come to a stop several feet before the white line. The shifter was still in first. I sat at the stop sign for several long moments, thinking.

Nob Hill is, of course, a hill. It is a tall and, even by San Francisco standards, rather steep hill. I realized that my species does not possess enough feet to properly execute the maneuver I was now presented with. I needed to simultaneously use the clutch, brake, and gas pedals. Unfortunate me, I had only two feet.

I decided just to try it. I took my foot off the brake. The car immediately started rolling down the hill.

I had to divide my attention between trying to make the pedals work and steering out of our trajectory parked cars and other obstacles. We had now rolled back about half a block and were rapidly gaining speed. I screeched on the brakes. At least, I thought, reduce our velocity. I was having horrible visions of rolling into Chinatown backwards in a stolen Ferrari totally out of control with a Tristanian lobster fisherman as my accomplice.

I let the clutch out as I stepped on the gas, not so hard this time. When we got to the top of the hill, I blew off the stop sign, making a left turn past Grace Cathedral and the Fairmont Hotel without even slowing down. One block away, on California Street, I made a right and we were on the Drive.

Walt enjoyed riding in the car tremendously. He naturally understood the rhythm of traveling. He adjusted to the pace of the Drive, knowing exactly when to look for the next sign.

When we got to the Palace of the Legion of Honor we stopped to get out and look at the Holocaust memorial. Of all the epic statuary to forgotten glories in the City, this simple memorial is by far the most effective. I have no idea if the Second World War involved Tristan de Cunha, but Walt knew nothing about it. I explained to him a little bit of the history and why people felt memorials to be necessary.

By this time it was getting on towards later in the day. I have very fair skin and I constantly have to worry about getting sunburned. I thought that by now, with the sun reaching a lower angle relative to the horizon, it might be an excellent time to put the top down on the car.

We found the catches for the release and released them. I took hold of the leading edge of the roof and pushed it towards the rear of the car. This all went very smoothly until the roof was about halfway down. Then it got stuck. We pushed and pulled and prodded and cajoled the roof, but we could not get it to go down any further. When we tried putting the roof back up, we found that it no longer fit properly. We had resigned ourselves to driving around with the roof stuck half open and half closed.

Walt got in the car first. It was than that he noticed a metal bar running underneath the fabric top. Further investigation revealed a way to remove the bar. When we had done this, the top went down the rest of the way effortlessly.

I stepped back several steps to admire our handiwork. Something still did not look right. The top was still attached to the rear portion of the car. I examined this and found that it was attached to the body of the car with a series of snaps. It took much pulling and grunting, but these, too, finally gave way.

I was beginning to like the Ferrari. We drove off in more style than I had ever imagined possible.

I felt that my competence was rapidly increasing. I was not afraid of the car as I had been just an hour or two before. Even the shifting was becoming familiar and easy. The only problem was that I had never had a chance to use any gear higher than second.

I knew I would have an opportunity soon, though. I paid almost no attention to the part of the drive we were on, so intently was I focusing on the part to come.

After the drive goes down Army Street, it takes a jog through the not-really-all-that-scenic Bayview district. From there it goes onto Highway 280. This is the part I was anticipating. This freeway has been closed since the earthquake. Thoughtfully, a two mile section of it has remained open almost exclusively for the purpose of the 49 Mile Drive. This stretch of road is utterly barren and devoid of traffic at any hour of the day or night. Of all the places to be in a Ferrari in San Francisco, this was undoubtedly the best.

When we finally came to the on-ramp I could barely contain myself. I briefly explained to Walt what was going to happen: we were going to go very, very fast. The speedometer went up to 160. I wondered how fast the car would actually be able to go.

The light changed and I jammed on the accelerator.

I have always been disappointed by airplanes. Somehow distance takes all the reality out of speed. Yes, an airplane may be cruising at 400 mph, but at 40,000 feet it seems to be just barely crawling along. The scenery inches by agonizingly slowly. Even at takeoff and landing the sensations of speed and power are minimized.

I was not disappointed by the Ferrari. The acceleration pinned my body against the seat, my head forced into the cradle of the headrest. I imagined, or think I imagined, little waves in the flesh of my cheeks. I had to grip the ball of the shifter tight in my right hand and not let go. I was sure that if I did my arm would be flung to my side and I would never be able to force it out against the force.

At the one mile mark we were doing 118 mph and I still had the car in fourth gear. I shifted and we leapt forward. At one and one half miles, we had attained 156 mph and I was afraid to go any faster. I also remembered that in half a mile we would have to deal with a swerve, a stoplight, train tracks, and a city street. I decided to start slowing down now.

After we had negotiated the stoplight, I pulled the car over, killed the engine, and got out. I had started trembling when I first brought the car back down under 100 mph. By now my shaking would best be described as convulsions. I lay on my back in a patch of dirt, unable to keep from thrashing on the ground. I felt sharp rocks poking me in the back, weeds and stickers getting into my socks. Only after several minutes of hyperventilation was I able to stop shaking. Finally I was able to get back on my feet.

I decided we needed a temporary break from the Drive. I pulled around the corner to a donut shop that I knew would be open. It always was. It took about half an hour of drinking cups of strong black coffee and eating jelly-filleds before I felt ready to get back in the car.

Walt had seemed remarkably unperturbed throughout this entire encounter, but he did seem to enjoy the donuts. I was so caught up in myself that I realized that a jelly donut was yet another in a long string of firsts for him.

By the time we had gotten back to where we had started on the Drive, for it runs in a loop, the sky was on the indeterminate edge between dusk and full dark. I turned off California, went down a block, then turned left onto Sacramento. This was the same hill we had rolled backwards down only a few hours before. In some ways I was hesitant to give the car back, it had been lots of fun to drive. But then I imagined trying to park a Ferrari in my neighborhood. That would simply not do. There are some types of insults of being that are too much for people to excuse. A car like that parked outside my building would be an affront to everyone who lived there. The urge to kick out a window or scratch the paint or stab a tire would be too great.

Besides, keeping the car would violate my tacit agreement with Jose, and would probably get me in a lot of trouble. Police Headquarters is located at Seventh and Bryant, about four blocks from my place, and I do not think it would take them too long to find me if they set their minds to it.

This mental deliberation took well under a block of traveling up the hill. The garage was rapidly approaching me on my right. Even from this distance, I could hear a great commotion coming from inside. The noises were not any that I really could identify, but I did not like the sound of them.

Amazingly, miraculously, there was a parking spot just outside the garage. I cut the lights and turned off the engine while we were still rolling, hoping to come in unnoticed. This was a brilliant plan, but I had forgotten one thing. The steering wheel locked up as soon as the key was turned off. We hit the curb quite a bit harder then I had intended, and the front end of the car went up onto the sidewalk diagonally. That was not exactly what I had in mind, but it would do. I yanked on the emergency brake and jumped out over the door of the car. I whispered to Walt to be quiet and follow me.

We walked down the hill about half a block before crossing the street. We then walked back up the hill. Instinctively I knew that this was probably a bad idea, but I had to find out what was going on inside the garage.

When we had reached to a point where we could see inside, I could hardly believe my eyes. A whole group of men with shaved heads dressed in purple robes and yellow sashes seemed to have invaded the garage. Jose was surrounded by these men, many of whom were playing drums or cymbals or long alp-horn-looking things. The rest were chanting and droning in a most peculiar way.

There was also a very distraught woman there. She did

not seem to be on the same mission as the men with the shaved heads. She wore a tailored linen suit and several strands of pearls. She was screaming.

I looked at Walt and he looked at me. Walt's system had rapidly become accustomed to being shocked. Any one day in San Francisco could provide him with several lifetimes worth of stories to tell back on Tristan, if anyone would listen. This scene, as we both could tell immediately, went well beyond our normal level of everyday weirdness. I knew I was curious, but I could not tell what Walt was feeling.

He was halfway across the street before I decided that I wanted to go over there, too.

As we crossed the street I had a difficult time picking out what the woman was screaming, but when I did I was glad that Jose had created a diversion for us. She was nearly incoherent, shouting that no one could seem to find her Ferrari, her beautiful Ferrari. She shouted about her being a dermatologist, and a good dermatologist at that. She had gone to school for twelve years to become a world-class authority on zits. Her education was wasted, she said, on pimply teens. Her research had gotten her nowhere, the only thing she needed to know for her practice was how to spell benzoyl peroxide, and whether to recommend a 5% or 10% dosage. The stuff did not even require a prescription.

She was really losing it. She went on to say, or scream rather, that her one joy in life, her single consolation for a lifetime of healing acne sufferers was her Ferrari, and now it was GONE!!! The last word came out more as a howl than an articulate word. She was sobbing hysterically now, a splatter of tears streaking her glasses.

This was not going to be easy.

We had been in the garage for few minutes now, and I had given practically all my attention to the yelling lady dermatologist whose Ferrari we had used. I was startled when I noticed Walt had gone off somewhere by himself. I looked around and spotted him speaking to one of the men in robes. I went over to join them.

The man was speaking very excitedly, and in a very thick accent, but I was able to get the gist of what he was saying. He claimed that Jose, King of the Parking Lot was in fact the Panchen Lama, the second-highest ranking member of the Tibetan Buddhist hierarchy.

I was skeptical. The monk, at least that is what he told me he was, said that the Panchen Lama had left Tibet at the same time the more famous Dalai Lama had. They both served for several years during the 1950's on the Steering Committee of the People's Republic of China. The Dalai Lama had left his Panchen colleague in China for a return to Tibet before finally settling in exile in India.

Until today, the Panchen Lama had never been heard from again. The authorities in Beijing had claimed for years that the Lama had stayed in China and renounced his vows as a monk. Government reports claimed that he had married and started a family, and was a very loyal communist.

The monks claimed that all this was untrue. They said that this Jose/Panchen person had escaped from China and come to San Francisco. For an unknown number of years he had held a job as a parking lot attendant to conceal his identity.

I asked the monk how they knew to come here to look for their long lost leader. His answer really scared me. He said that the abbot of their monastery in Dharamsala, India had heard strange music in his head that reminded him of the Panchen Lama. He instructed this group of monks to come here to San Francisco to look for him. They had found him in only six weeks of wandering around the City.

That did it; it was time to get out of there.

I went over to the dermatologist and tried to get her attention. I was altogether most anxious to leave that garage far behind me forever. I was not very patient with the screaming doctor. When she finally looked at me I told her that these Tibetan Monks could often be part of miraculous occurrences. I suggested that she look around, and maybe even outside, to see if her Ferrari had somehow materialized since they had arrived.

With that I grabbed Walt by the sleeve of his sweater and we both took off running down the hill.

XIV

WALT HAD DONE SO WELL with the Drive that I decided to take him riding on the N Judah the next day. I thought the form of riding meditation would be good for him, and it certainly was cheap enough.

We had already been out walking for several hours when we caught the N at the corner of Cole and Carl in the Haight-Ashbury. We rode out towards the beach. I had long since modulated the intensity of the transmitter, but Walt and I still spent most of our time in silence. We rode together, looking out the window.

I became interested in the scenery inside the car, the ebb and flow of the people, while Walt watched the streets go by outside the window. Passengers got on and got off, but we stayed in our seats, going all the way to the turn-around at the extreme edge of North America.

The train turned around and headed back across the city. The reassuring clack of the wheels helped me to attain the state that I always seem to reach on Muni. My head felt at the same time heavy and very clear. In my unattention, I was acutely aware of everything occurring in the City. It was an exhilarating feeling and the streets passed quickly.

It should be noted here that the Muni in San Francisco runs both above and below ground. Downtown, where traffic is the most condensed and space is at a premium, the trains run in subway tunnels. As they go out into the neighborhoods, the trains pop up from the ground and run like streetcars. It is a nice system.

I probably should have paid more attention to the fact that, as we went on, more and more people seemed to be getting off the train. Normally an inbound train gets progressively more crowded as it comes in from the beach. Our train was an exception. By the time we got to the mouth of the tunnel, Walt and I were the only ones aboard except for the driver, whom we could not see.

I took in the rising clatter of the wheels as we began our descent. I have always enjoyed the way the train gently rocks back and forth, having to find its footing, so to speak, as if it had never been underground before.

We had only been underground a few moments when Walt fell out of his seat. It was not too unusual for him to do something like this, but I knew immediately that this was different. He lay flat on his back, rigid somehow. Pivoting on his ankles, his body swung into an upright position; a motion of which no human, even a Tristanian lobster fisherman, is capable.

At that point I became aware of another presence on the streetcar. Something like a person or a group of people, but somehow neither, was in front of us in the aisle. No one had gotten on or off the train for the last three stops. This amalgamation in front of us, again I want to call it a person or people, though it obviously was not human, had made some kind of dramatic contact with Walt.

Walt's eyes were fixed on the ever-shifting mass. Walt appeared to be engrossed in some sort of deep conversation. He had the expression that I had seen a number of times on the faces of very learned men and women at parties when, engrossed at last in some tremendously serious academic conversation after several hours of frivolity, with the slightest bead of a drink hanging from the lower lip, they breathe in, fix the gaze, and prepare to expound.

Walt's mouth never opened. He just maintained the expression of thought ready to spring into action. It/they seemed to be concentrating its/their attention(s) on Walt. I was being ignored.

As quickly as the interchange had begun, it ended. The whole thing lasted no more than fifteen seconds. I would have attributed it entirely to the sorts of hallucinations that occasionally accompany my meditations on the train but for the fact that Walt fell back again, hitting his head rather hard on the floor.

Walt was still barely conscious when I hustled him off at the next station, Castro Street and got him up the escalator and into a cab. He passed out just blocks from home.

XV

I T TOOK SEVERAL DAYS of talking and piecing together
before I really understood at all that had occurred in
the tunnel. I realize that I may never quite get all of the
parts together perfectly, but the following is the basis of
what Walt told me.

Walt had been contacted by an alien intelligence. This
race did not exist as individuals or groups as we understand the term. In the mass of information relayed to Walt
during this short encounter, no attempt to elucidate this
point was made. The race was called the Easybeats.

For many of our years, the Easybeats had been involved
in an experiment similar to my own. The main function
of their entire society was to search for intelligent life
through the use of music. So far, and this after a very long
time, they had not found any.

They had left their standard beacon "Friday on my
Mind" on Earth some years before. By rebroadcasting this
song, I was in effect relaying their signal. It was the first
lead that they had had in over five hundred grolnoks. Walt
was not able to tell me just how long a grolnok was, but he
assured we that it was a very long time indeed.

The Easybeats had come to Earth immediately to investigate my signal. But, of course, the signal I was broadcasting was not penetrating the atmosphere. They only received the transmission after it had been relayed by Walt's elaborate dental work.

Thus had they come to the conclusion that, themselves excepted, Walt was the only intelligent life-form in the universe. Walt said that the Easybeats were more different from us than any human could imagine. Their perception of life, and especially of humans, was much different than any of us would have expected. The Easybeats had an apartment. They even had a job. Still, all this interaction with humans had not convinced them that our species even qualified as a life form, let alone an intelligent one.

The Easybeats could only live underground. They felt sure that exposure to the surface of the planet would be instantly fatal. Thus they found the basement on Tehama alley. They had also, in a fit of exuberance, found a job at the all-night Japanese poolhall. The Easybeats were fantastically adept at tunneling. They had quickly established a network of tunnels leading from their basement apartment to the poolhall. They had also made extensive use of the tunnels belonging to the Municipal Railway, even going as far as hiding their space vehicle in a seldom-used shaft at the Embarcadero Station. They had apologized for not making direct contact sooner, but Walt had not previously gone underground.

They also gave the impression of being highly *impatiens*. They told Walt that they had left their home planet as soon as they received his message. This seems to have been about the time he initially boarded the *San Geronimo*. They were able to extrapolate from his course that he was headed for San Francisco, so they came here and got ready to meet him. They were irate when his magnetic field started to throw the ship's navigational instruments off. Unwilling to move to a new city, they instead contacted him in his sleep to give him a revised, and not quite so agonizingly slow, course.

They had also invited Walt to return with them to their home world. This seemed to them to be a reasonable offer; that the universe's two sentient species should cohabitate. They said that they realized such a decision would take some deliberation on his part. If he wanted to go with the Easybeats, all he had to do was show up at the Embarcadero Station in seven days. If he were not there, they would leave without him. They did not explain why they were not willing to be more patient.

I was alarmed. I was alarmed that I believed Walt's crazy story unquestioningly. I was alarmed that he was taking seriously their offer to go to their home planet. I was not alarmed, but I was jealous and somewhat angry that, if it had not been for wave-skip phenomena and some half-baked lobster fisherman's dental work, the Easybeats would now be considering me the universe's only other sentient life form instead of Walt. It must be said. I was pissed.

XVI

AND SO OUR DAYS WERE almost gone. Walt had of course decided to go. I felt that he had not really given his home planet a chance. I had not even had a chance to show him some of my favorite parts of San Francisco. I had learned to see in Walt the sort of stoic determination that had allowed his family to fish the same patch of water for seven generations. I did not believe that I could change Walt's mind.

Walt had little to do to get ready. He had nothing to pack, no one to see, nothing to sell, no house except mine to move out of. His was to be perhaps the simplest departure ever.

Finally the final day came. Walt and I had a big lunch at a Burmese restaurant called Real Good Karma on Dolores Street. I felt dolorous myself. I had come to respect Walt somewhat. We had both felt feelings for each other that we had never felt before. We were friends.

We walked up to the Church Street Station. We hopped the first inbound train that came down the tunnel, a K Ingleside. Walt was carrying under one arm his duffle bag with the few wool sweaters that refused to fit on his body. In his other hand was his lunchbox. I did not know just how I would explain its absence to my roommate, but I had to let him take it. He was the only passenger on the train wearing rubber boots.

Once again, passengers got off at each stop, but none got on to replace them. A palpable tension built in the car. Few people were visible on the platforms as we pulled through each of the stations.

Embarcadero Station was completely empty when we pulled in. I noticed that our train had no driver. I wondered idly how long it had been running itself. The Station was, as always, gently lit with tasteful mood lighting. We got off the train and walked around the deserted platform. I enjoyed hearing my footsteps echo off the convex-tiled walls.

We had only been there a few moments when the unknowable form of the Easybeats rambled out of the tunnel. They made contact with Walt in some way that I could not perceive. He turned agilely on one heel and floated gently off the platform and down the tunnel, following slightly behind them.

I ran to the escalator, ran up the moving stairs three or four at a time. I pushed my way through the turnstile, where there was still no one around, and out into the street. There was no traffic. No idle robber barons happened by from the financial district. Not a single longshoreman or tourist was to be seen anywhere.

I believe that I was the only one to see the brown sphere with no windows, looking very much like a small meteor, rise up from somewhere near the Ferry Building.

I watched it shoot across the Bay, climbing, always climbing, until I lost track of it.

I took a long time walking home that day.

XVII

S INCE WALT LEFT I HAVE been in contact with several
people on Tristan. It was difficult for me to come up
with a believable story about how I knew Walt and what
happened to him after he left.

As far as anyone on his native island knows, he died
on board ship, my ship, shortly after I rescued him. I was
sailing alone in a race around the world. Rescuing Walt
and looking after him dropped me out of competition. I
was horribly distraught when he died. In this elaborate lie,
I buried Walt at sea.

Mrs. Wilkins has been very kind in her letters and
has invited me to come and stay with her. I suspect that
she could use some help in raising the twins. Perhaps she
could help me learn some more music on the piano, if I
have time. I have a job waiting there for me, of course.
Someone needs to carry on the respectable tradition of
fishing Walt's ancestral waters in his father's boat.

I even satisfy the ultimate test of a Tristanian fisherman: I have never tasted lobster. My mother is horribly al-
lergic to it, to the point that eating it could kill her. Since
she and I share most of the same allergies, I have never

dared to try it.

I have not yet made up my mind as to whether or not I will set up my transmitter on Tristan.

AUTHOR'S DISCLAIMER

Walt is a work of fiction which takes generous liberties with reality. The reader would be poorly advised to take any portion of this book as factual in areas including, but not limited to: fishing, navigation, bacteriology, manual transmissions, and investing in vintage lunch boxes. Most importantly, the frame of a grand piano would make a highly inefficient broadcast antenna for all sorts of reasons. During the gestation of this book, many people including the experts at G. Leuenberger Pianos, the *San Francisco Chronicle* and Ferrari of San Francisco generously shared their knowledge, which I ignored as often as not. Factual inconsistencies are therefore solely my responsibility.

—IS